Little Red Riding Hood

A Tale about Staying Safe

Retold by Suzanne Gaffney Beason
Illustrated by Walter Velez

Reader's Digest Young Families

Once upon a time, there was a sweet little girl whose grandmother had made her a red cape with a hood. Everywhere she went, she was called Little Red Riding Hood.

One day Little Red Riding Hood's mother said to her, "Your grandmother is not feeling well. Please bring her this bread and this dish of butter. Go straight to her house and do not dawdle along the way."

As Little Red Riding Hood strolled through the woods, she met a wolf. He wanted to eat her right then, but he dared not, because some woodcutters were working nearby.

"Where are you going?" asked the wicked wolf.

"To see my grandmother," she replied, not knowing that it was dangerous to speak to a wolf. "She lives beyond this forest in the next village. Her house is the first one you come to."

"Well, now," said the cunning wolf, "why don't I visit your grandmother, too? I'll take this path, and you take that one, and we will see who gets there first."

The wolf set off running with all his might by the shorter road, and the little girl continued on her merry way by the longer road.

As Little Red Riding Hood wandered down the path, she amused herself by gathering nuts, chasing after butterflies, and making bouquets of wildflowers.

The wolf quickly arrived at the grandmother's house. He knocked on the old woman's door.

"Who is there?" asked the grandmother.

"It is your granddaughter, Little Red Riding Hood," said the wolf, disguising his voice. "I've come to see how you are. I've brought you some bread and a little dish of butter from my mother."

"How wonderful," said the grandmother, who was resting in bed. "Lift the latch and open the door."

The wolf did just as the old woman had instructed. He lifted the latch, and the door flew open.

As soon as the wolf entered, the grandmother could see that this was not Little Red Riding Hood. When she realized it was a wolf, she fainted with fright.

The wolf quickly picked up the old woman and put her in a nearby closet.

Next, the wolf put on one of the grandmother's nightgowns and one of her caps to disguise himself. He crawled into the bed and waited patiently for Little Red Riding Hood to arrive.

At last, there came a knock at the door.

"Who is there?" asked the wolf, knowing very well it was Little Red Riding Hood.

When Little Red Riding Hood heard the wolf's gruff voice, she was startled. But thinking that her grandmother had a bad cold, she replied, "It is Little Red Riding Hood, your granddaughter. I've brought you some bread and a dish of butter from my mother."

"Come in, dear. Put the bread and the little dish of butter on the chair," said the wolf. "Then come sit on the bed with me."

Little Red Riding Hood did as she was told and placed the bread and the little dish of butter on the chair. Then she took off her beautiful red cape.

As Little Red Riding Hood came toward her grandmother's old feather bed, the wolf pulled the covers up tightly under his chin. When Little Red Riding Hood climbed onto the bed, she was amazed by her grandmother's appearance.

"Oh, Grandmother, what big ears you have!" exlaimed Little Red Riding Hood.

"All the better to hear you with, my dear!" said the wolf.

"And Grandmother," Little Red Riding Hood continued, "what big eyes you have!"

"All the better to see you with!" said the wolf.

"But Grandmother, what big teeth you have!" said Little Red Riding Hood.

"All the better to EAT you with!" cried the wolf as he leaped from the bed. Just as the wolf was about to gobble up Little Red Riding Hood, he slipped on the bedspread and fell down. Little Red Riding Hood escaped through the door.

Inside the closet, the grandmother awoke with a start. She grabbed a broom and a skillet and chased the wolf right out the door. He was never seen again!

After the wolf was gone, Little Red Riding Hood ran back to her grandmother. When she was sure her grandmother was fine, she ran all the way home. She didn't stop once. For you see, Little Red Riding Hood had learned this very important lesson:

Little ones, this seems to say,
Never stop upon your way.
As you're witty, so be wise;
Wolves may lurk in every guise.
Now as then, 'tis simple truth—
Sweetest tongue has sharpest tooth!

Famous Fables, Lasting Virtues Tips for Parents

Now that you've read *Little Red Riding Hood*, use these pages as a guide to teach your child the virtues in the story. By talking about the story and its message and engaging in the activities, you can help your child develop good judgment and a strong moral character.

About Staying Safe

Teaching our children not to talk to strangers can be a challenge. After all, children see us talking to strangers all the time—a cashier at a store or a mother at a playground. And telling the difference between a "bad" and "good" stranger on the basis of appearance is often impossible, even for grown-ups. How can we teach our children to stay safe without filling them with undue fear or anxiety? Here are some suggestions:

1. *Important information.* Children as young as four years old can be taught their telephone number with area code, home address, and the full names of their parents. They can also learn to dial 911 in case of an emergency. Discuss with your child what to do if she gets lost or separated from you in a public place. A good rule to follow is to find a policeman, a store clerk, or a mother with young children. These are usually safe people to ask for help.

2. *Strangers.* Little Red Riding Hood does not realize that the wolf is a dangeous-looking stranger. But do "bad guys" always look dangerous? Talk with your child about how it is impossible to tell if people are good or bad by the way they look. Teach your child to pay attention to her feelings and to use her common sense—if she's scared, she should look for help. Practice the safety rules you've taught.

3. *Run, yell, tell.* Teach your child to be cautious. He should not go anywhere with a stranger, even if the stranger asks for help. Explain that grown-ups should ask other grown-ups for help, not a child. If a stranger tries to harm your child, instruct him to run, yell, and tell—*run* away, *yell* for help ("This is not my mommy/daddy!"), and *tell* a safe grown-up right away.